Good to be small

Good to be small

Sean Cassidy

Fitzhenry & Whiteside

Design by Wycliffe Smith Design Inc.

Published in Canada by Fitzhenry & Whiteside, 195 Allstate Parkway, Markham, Ontario L3R 4T8

Published in the United States by Fitzhenry & Whiteside, 121 Harvard Avenue, Suite 2, Allston, Massachusetts 02134

www.fitzhenry.ca   godwit@fitzhenry.ca.

10 9 8 7 6 5 4 3 2 1

National Library of Canada Cataloguing in Publication

Cassidy, Sean, 1947-
Good to be small / by Sean Cassidy ; illustrated by Sean Cassidy.

ISBN 1-55041-734-7 (bound).--ISBN 1-55041-699-5 (pbk.)

I. Title.

PS8555.A78122G66 2002   jC813'.6   C2002-901502-2
PZ7

U.S. Publisher Cataloging-in-Publication Data
(Library of Congress Standards)

Good to be small / by Sean Cassidy ; illustrated by Sean Cassidy.—1st ed.
[32] p. : col. ill. ;   cm.
Summary: Mama Sheep calls out the alarm. Her lamb is missing! When little Mouse offers to find the lost lamb,
the other sheep dismiss her. But she doesn't mind. Sometimes the smallest member of the barnyard can get
the biggest results, and Mouse is about to prove it.
ISBN 1-55041-734-7

ISBN 1-55041-699-5 (pbk.)
1. Sheep – Fiction. 2. Size – Fiction. I. Title.
[E] 21   2002   AC CIP

Fitzhenry & Whiteside acknowledges with thanks the Canada Council for the Arts, the Government of Canada through the Book
Publishing Industry Development Program (BPIDP), and the Ontario Arts Council for their support for our publishing program.

Printed in Hong Kong

To Sylvia and Maggie
for your love and patience
S.C.

Something was wrong in the barnyard.
Mouse looked up from her dinner.
Mama Sheep was crying.

"Lamb, La-a-a-mb," she called.
"Where's my la-a-a-mb?"

"Lamb, La-a-a-mb," the other sheep bleated.
"Where's our la-a-a-mb?"

But no lamb ran to its mother's side.
Mouse scampered over to Mama Sheep.
"I can help find Lamb," she said.

The sheep shook their heads sadly.

"Too small, too sma-a-a-ll," they bleated.

"You'll see," said Mouse. "Sometimes it's good to be small."

And she climbed to the top of the barn.

On the roof, Mouse searched for Lamb.
Below, she saw Fox sneaking behind the barn.
Near the bridge she saw the turtles warming
their shells in the sun.

She saw the stream winding through the forest.
In the trees she saw Hawk making her nest.
In a small clearing, she spotted it.
"There's the lamb!" she cried.

Mouse slid down the roof of the barn.
She sailed into the air like a small bird.
She landed as softly as fur on Fox's back.
Fox didn't even know she was there.

"Run to the bridge," Mouse whispered.

Surprised, Fox raced down the road. Soon he was running so fast, his paws barely touched the ground.

Mouse held on tightly.

As Fox crossed the bridge, Mouse jumped. She
settled as lightly as a petal on Turtle's back.
Turtle didn't even know she was there.

"Swim down the stream," Mouse whispered.

Surprised, Turtle jumped into the water and floated downstream. Soon they were roaring through the rapids.

Mouse held on tightly.

As the water slowed, Mouse leaped to shore.
She crawled up Hawk's tree. She moved as quietly
as a breeze onto Hawk's back.

Hawk didn't even know she was there.

"Find Lamb," Mouse whispered.

Surprised, Hawk flapped her wings and rose
into the air. Soon they were soaring over
the treetops.

Mouse held on tightly.

As Hawk glided over Lamb, Mouse slid from her back.
She landed as gently as fluff on Lamb's fleece.
Lamb was happy to see her.

"Don't worry, Lamb," Mouse said gently. "You'll
soon be home."

Together they walked back through the woods.
They trotted along the stream. They crossed the bridge.
Soon they could see the farm.

"Lamb, La-a-a-mb," called the sheep. "There's
our la-a-a-mb!"

Lamb ran to the barnyard and crawled under the fence.
"Here's my la-a-a-mb!" sang Mama Sheep.
Mouse smiled. "Sometimes it is good to be small..."
she said,

"...except when happy sheep are around!"